KT-495-730

This book belongs to

....

I celebrated World Book Day with this
brilliant gift from my local bookseller,
Nosy Crow, Pamela Butchart and
Thomas Flintham.

CELEBRATE STORIES. LOVE READING.

This book has been specially written and published to celebrate **World Book Day**. We are a charity that offers every child and young person the opportunity to read and love books by offering you the chance to have a book of your own. To find out more – as well as oodles of fun activities and reading recommendations to continue your reading journey, visit **worldbookday.com**

World Book Day in the UK and Ireland is made possible by generous sponsorship from National Book Tokens, participating publishers, booksellers, authors and illustrators. The £1 book tokens are a gift from your local bookseller.*

World Book Day works in partnership with a number of charities, all of whom are working to encourage a love of reading for pleasure.

The National Literacy Trust is an independent charity that encourages children to enjoy reading. Just 10 minutes of reading every day can make a big difference to how well you do at school and to how successful you could be in life.
literacytrust.org.uk

The Reading Agency inspires people of all ages and backgrounds to read for pleasure and empowerment. They run the Summer Reading Challenge in partnership with libraries, as well as supporting reading groups in schools and libraries all year round. Find out more and join your local library.
summerreadingchallenge.org.uk

World Book Day also facilitates fundraising for:

Book Aid International, an international book donation and library development charity. Every year, they provide one million books to libraries and schools in communities where children would otherwise have little or no opportunity to read.
bookaid.org.uk

Read for Good, who motivate children in schools to read for fun through its sponsored read, which thousands of schools run on World Book Day and throughout the year. The money raised provides new books and resident storytellers in all of the UK's children's hospitals.
readforgood.org

*€1.50 in Ireland

THE BABY BROTHER FROM OUTER SPACE!

PAMELA BUTCHART

nosy crow

First published in the UK in 2018 by Nosy Crow Ltd
The Crow's Nest, 14 Baden Place, Crosby Row,
London, SE1 1YW, UK

Nosy Crow and associated logos are trademarks and/or registered
trademarks of Nosy Crow Ltd

Text copyright © Pamela Butchart, 2018
Cover and illustrations copyright © Thomas Flintham, 2018

The right of Pamela Butchart and Thomas Flintham to be identified
as the author and illustrator respectively of this work has been asserted
by them in accordance with the Copyright, Designs
and Patents Act 1988.

Printed and bound in the UK by Clays Ltd, St. Ives Plc

Papers used by Nosy Crow are made from wood grown in
sustainable forests.

ISBN: 978 1 78800 118 2

www.nosycrow.com

For The Bump,
who kicked all the way
through writing this book.
Love Mummy x
P. B.

For Bethany
T. F.

Look out for:

BABY ALIENS GOT MY TEACHER!

THE SPY WHO LOVED SCHOOL DINNERS

MY HEADTEACHER IS A VAMPIRE RAT!

ATTACK OF THE DEMON DINNER LADIES

TO WEE OR NOT TO WEE!

THERE'S A WEREWOLF IN MY TENT!

THE PHANTOM LOLLIPOP MAN!

We Need to Move School!

A **LOT** of **WEIRD STUFF** happens at our school and Jodi (that's my friend) says that we probably should have all left and gone to a **NEW SCHOOL** by now.

And I am beginning to think that she is **RIGHT** because it isn't really

1

NORMAL to have to deal with head teachers that turn into VAMPIRE RATS or DEMON DINNER LADIES who put EYEBALLS in your water jug at school dinners.

But this isn't the story about the time with the vampire rat OR the demon dinner ladies or even the time there was a WEREWOLF IN OUR TENT.

This is about the time a BABY came to our school from

OUTER SPACE.

And Zach (that's our other friend)

says we probably should have **KNOWN** something was going to go **SERIOUSLY WRONG** when the sky went **DARK** and that we should have **ALL** been wearing **BLU-TACK GOGGLES** like Maisie did because **ALIEN MIND CONTROL** is **SERIOUS**.

My friend Jodi says that we're **LUCKY TO BE ALIVE**. And she's **RIGHT** because who **KNOWS** how toxic an **ALIEN BABY POO** is?

And it just goes to show that when a baby who has his own **PHONE** comes to your school, you never know **WHAT'S** going to happen!

A VIP Visitor

On Monday when we turned up to assembly, Mr Graves, the head teacher, told us that a SPECIAL GUEST would be visiting our school.

Everyone GROANED because that's the sort of thing Mr Graves says when he means there's someone **BORING** coming to see us like a **SCHOOL INSPECTOR** or someone from the **COUNCIL**. And then he makes us all smile and behave much better than we normally do and all the teachers start acting strange and making us do weird lessons. Like the time Miss Jones made us all pretend to be **NUMBERS** and lie down on the classroom floor to make a sum instead of just writing it on the whiteboard like she normally does.

But then something **STRANGE** happened. Mr Graves went behind the big stage curtain and when he appeared again he had a **BABY** with him!

Everyone **STARED** at the baby because we had never seen a **BABY** at an assembly before and I didn't think babies were even **ALLOWED** at primary school!

6

Then Mr Graves said, "This is our VIP guest for the day. What a great opportunity for us all to learn about babies!"

I looked at Jodi and she looked at me because this was one of the

WEIRDEST

things Mr Graves had ever said at an assembly and it was probably even weirder than the time he said all the stuff about STRESS and PAPERWORK and then started crying a bit.

Then Zach said, "Who IS that

baby? Why is he a VIP?"

But I just shrugged because I had

NO IDEA

who the baby was or why he was so important that he needed to be coming to our school.

Then Mrs Akbar, our Year 3 teacher that we hadn't seen for ages, came on stage and said that it was HER BABY and that she was coming back to school next week and that she'd brought Samir in with her for the day to see how we were all getting on.

EVERYONE turned and looked

at Haroon in Year 5 because we knew that Mrs Akbar was his **MUM** and that the **VIP BABY** must be his **BABY BROTHER.**

That's when Jodi said that there was **NO WAY** she was changing a nappy. And we all knew she said that because she'd had a **TRAUMATIC NAPPY EXPERIENCE** when she was staying in a caravan with her aunt and her baby cousin. And Jodi said that the

☆ — EXPLODING — ☆
NAPPY

had been **SO BAD** that they'd

actually had to move caravans and that she still had **NIGHTMARES** about it.

Then Maisie started rocking backwards and forwards and saying that she was **TERRIFIED** of babies, especially **VIP ONES**, and that she was going to have to get her mum to come and pick her up.

But then Mrs Akbar came down from the stage and ALL of the teachers RAN past us towards the baby. And I actually had to pull my foot in a bit and shout, "HEY!" because one of them almost stood RIGHT on my toe.

That's when Zach said, "This is WEIRD. The teachers are going

MAD for the baby!"

And he was RIGHT because all the teachers had ABANDONED their classes and were crowding round the baby, making weird sounds and faces at it and even the OFFICE LADIES were smiling (and they NEVER smile, not even when you say thank you FIVE TIMES when they eventually answer one of your questions).

But then Maisie tugged on my sleeve and pointed to Haroon and I saw that he was still sitting on the floor, looking down at his hands. And he looked MISERABLE.

Zach said that it was probably because he was embarrassed about his mum being on stage and that if HIS mum was up there he'd lock himself in the toilets because there was NO WAY she wouldn't want to sing into the microphone and maybe even do one of her DANCE ROUTINES.

But I didn't think Haroon WAS embarrassed about his mum being on stage because his mum had worked at our school for years and there wasn't really anything to be embarrassed about because everyone LOVED Mrs Akbar and she'd never done any dance routines at us before or anything like that.

So we all went over to Haroon and asked him if he was OK.

And THAT'S when we saw the

WEIRD LOOK

on his face.

So we all sat down next to him and I put my hand on his shoulder and said, "Haroon. What's wrong? You can tell us."

Haroon took a deep breath and looked up.

And then he said, "It's my baby brother. I think he's from

OUTER SPACE!"

Weird Alien Language

Maisie fainted INSTANTLY because she is TERRIFIED of aliens and one time when we thought our teacher, Miss Jones, was an alien she actually fainted HEAD FIRST into her shepherd's pie at school dinners. That's how scared she was.

So me and Zach picked Maisie up by an arm and a leg each and Jodi said, "DEN. NOW!"

But I said, "What about Haroon?" because it's only me and Jodi and Zach and Maisie that know about The Den and are allowed to have

SECRET MEETINGS

there. So Jodi turned and looked Haroon **RIGHT IN THE EYE** and said, "Haroon of Year 5. Do you swear to keep the location of The Den a secret for **LIFE?**"

Haroon's eyes went wide and he nodded loads.

And Jodi said, "Good. Follow us."

When we got to The Den, Haroon looked

And I knew it was because he'd had **NO IDEA** that the cupboard under the stairs that go up to the boys' toilets was our **DEN** and also because we had to put Maisie in the

RECOVERY POSITION and wrap her in her SHOCK BLANKET while she drank a Ribena through a straw for STRENGTH.

Haroon sat down on one of the buckets we use for chairs and asked us if any of the teachers knew about The Den. So Jodi told him that they DEFINITELY DIDN'T and then she made him sign a piece of paper

and said it was

LEGALLY BINDING

which meant that if he ever told anyone about The Den he would go to jail because her mum's boyfriend's aunt was a LAWYER.

As soon as Haroon signed the paper, Jodi took out the OFFICIAL MINI-WHITEBOARD and pen that we use for all our secret meetings and Zach made Haroon a cup of tea.

Haroon was

MEGA IMPRESSED

that we had a kettle and tea and even some biscuits in The Den. But then he realised that the kettle doesn't work and that we don't have any milk and that we just use cold water from the tap and he didn't seem that impressed any more.

So anyway, that's when we asked Haroon to tell us EVERYTHING about his baby brother. And he told us that there was something

— SERIOUSLY SUSPICIOUS —

about Samir and that he wasn't a NORMAL HUMAN BABY and

that he suspected he had ALIEN POWERS.

Then Haroon told us that his mum had been acting like SOMEONE ELSE since the baby arrived and that she kept forgetting things, like to pick him up from football practice, or to finish a sentence that she was just saying, or to put TWO MARSHMALLOWS in his hot chocolate instead of just one.

Haroon said that his mum used to spend AGES asking him about school when they were having their dinner and that now she just ate her dinner really quickly and didn't really speak and that as SOON as the baby made any sound at ALL she would jump up and run over to see what he wanted.

Then Haroon looked RIGHT at me and said, "I'm pretty sure my baby brother is

CONTROLLING HER MIND."

So Jodi wrote "MIND CONTROL" on the whiteboard and I nodded to Haroon that he should keep going.

THAT'S when Haroon gulped and got a STRANGE LOOK on his face.

So I patted his shoulder and said it was OK and that there

23

was **NOTHING** he could tell us that would shock us because we dealt with stuff like this all the time and that we were practically **PROFESSIONALS.**

Haroon nodded and said, "It happens at night. I can't sleep."

And **THAT'S** when I noticed the **DARK CIRCLES** under Haroon's eyes.

I looked at Zach and he looked at Jodi because we had **NO IDEA** what Haroon was about to say.

And then he said, "He waits until Mum and Dad are asleep. And then he starts **TALKING.**"

And we all

GASPED!

Haroon said that it sounded like his baby brother was just babbling made-up nonsense but that he was sure it was an actual

ALIEN LANGUAGE!

Jodi let out a deep breath, which is what she sometimes does when she needs to FOCUS and STAY CALM.

And then she said, "Who do you think your baby brother is speaking to, Haroon?"

And Haroon looked at us all with **WIDE EYES** and pointed up to the roof.

And then he said, "I think he's speaking to

OUTER SPACE!"

Mind Control

When the bell went for the end of assembly, we all RAN back to the hall but it was already EMPTY.

Jodi said we'd better get to class QUICK before Miss Jones noticed so we started running along the corridor and THAT'S when Mrs

Seith (the deputy head teacher)
caught us and shouted, "HALT!"
and we all gasped because Mrs
Seith is SERIOUSLY SCARY and I
heard that one time she made every
single pupil in the school cry during

an assembly just by making her eyes go really WIDE.

Maisie GRABBED my hand and I could feel that she was shaking and I knew that we had to come up with a BELIEVABLE excuse for why we were out of class ASAP. But I am not very good at coming up with lies on the spot and Zach is even WORSE so I was just about to nudge Jodi so that SHE'D make something up when Haroon said, "We're here to find you, Miss. My mum, erm, I mean Mrs Akbar, wondered if you'd like to meet my baby brother? She's in my classroom just now."

We all STARED at Mrs Seith and I was ONE HUNDRED PER CENT sure she wasn't going to believe Haroon because it didn't really make sense that we'd all come to find her because me and Zach and Jodi aren't even IN Haroon's class and also because there's a

STRICT RULE

that pupils can only go in TWOS to deliver a message and that you have to have an OUT OF CLASS PASS (and we definitely didn't have one of those).

But then the WEIRDEST THING happened. Mrs Seith DIDN'T start shouting or give us a detention. She started smiling. LOADS! And she even did a bit of a giggling thing (which was TOTALLY creepy and Maisie squeezed my hand so tight I almost yelped).

Mrs Seith said that she'd LOVE to come and meet the baby and then she rushed us along the corridor and up the stairs. And I'm sure she was taking the stairs two at a time because I had to actually run a bit just to keep up with her.

☆

Haroon said Mrs Seith spent AGES with the baby, and then at break we saw her walk out the big doors and into the PLAYGROUND. She walked over to where baby Samir was sitting on a blanket on the grass with Mrs Akbar and as SOON as Samir saw her he put his hands in the air and she PICKED HIM UP. Then Samir pointed his chubby arm towards where the Year 6s were playing football and Mrs Seith took him over to watch.

That's when Zach gasped and said, "MIND CONTROL."

And we all nodded because it was

like the baby had sent a

MIND MESSAGE

all the way to Mrs Seith's office that he wanted her to come out to the playground and take him to watch the football game!

Then Zach said, "I think I know what's happening. The baby must think Mrs Seith is the most **POWERFUL** person in the school. That's why he's picked **HER** to do his bidding!"

And that made sense because even though Mr Graves is the head

teacher, Mrs Seith ACTS like she's
the head teacher and I'm pretty sure
Mr Graves is a tiny bit scared of her.

Zach said that we needed to get
CLOSER to see if there were any
signs of

in Mrs Seith's eyes, like if they'd
changed COLOUR or

gone COMPLETELY WHITE.

But when we got closer we saw that
Mrs Seith had put SUNGLASSES

ON and that's when we knew for SURE she was having her mind controlled by Haroon's baby brother and that he was probably the one who told her to put the sunglasses on in the first place.

Maisie raised a shaky finger and pointed at the baby and said, "Look. He's STARING at something."

And he WAS staring at something. He was staring at Gary Petrie, who was standing eating a bag of crisps instead of trying to get the ball (which is what he always does because he's not very good at football).

Then all of a sudden something UNBELIEVABLE happened. Gary Petrie got GOOD. He managed to get the ball away from the other team and kicked it REALLY hard into the goal before the goalkeeper even knew what was happening and everyone shouted, "GOOOOOOOOOAAAAAL!" and lifted him up into the air because he had just scored the WINNER!

That's when Haroon turned to us
and said, "See. I told you. He's got

ALIEN
POWERS."

I looked over at the baby and even
though I can't prove it I am almost
one hundred per cent sure that he
winked at us.

Babies are
From MARS!

After break, Miss Jones said it was time for baby Samir to visit OUR class. So Maisie made a pair of goggles out of Blu Tack and put them on because she said that she didn't want the baby to CONTROL HER MIND.

Jodi said that we all had to be

COMPLETELY
AWARE
OF OURSELVES

which meant that if we felt like we were getting really good or really bad at anything all of a sudden, like spelling or drawing or breathing, then we should say something **RIGHT AWAY** because it might be the baby controlling us with his

ALIEN
POWERS.

Then Jodi took a tissue out of her pocket and started stuffing bits up her nose and I knew that she was doing it because she was scared that there might be a NAPPY INCIDENT.

Then all of a sudden there was a knock at the door and Miss Jones RAN to answer it.

We all STARED as Mrs Akbar walked in with baby Samir and sat down at the table next to us.

I tried not to make EYE CONTACT with the baby but it was hard because he was facing me and then all of a sudden he looked RIGHT

AT ME and smiled and I got such a fright I covered my eyes with my hands and slammed my head down on the desk.

But then Miss Jones came over and asked what was wrong with me and why Maisie had Blu Tack stuck to her eyes so Jodi said that we both had headaches and that we were just trying different things to get rid of them. And Miss Jones said OK and to let her know if we needed to go to the nurse and Jodi said thanks.

I waited until a few minutes had passed before I lifted my head back up and when I did I saw that the baby was now at the other end of the room playing on the Reading Rug. But then I started to PANIC because everything looked more **BLURRY** than it had before the baby smiled at me and I was worried that he had

ZAPPED MY EYES

or something. But then after about a minute my eyes went back to normal and I realised that it had just been because I'd had them shut so tight.

Then all of a sudden Jodi pointed to the baby and said, "**LOOK!** He's **DOING** something."

And he WAS. The baby had ABC BLOCKS and it looked like he was concentrating REALLY HARD.

Jodi got up and said that she needed to sharpen her pencil even though she didn't and we weren't even supposed to be using our pencils because we were supposed to be discussing what we knew about BABIES in a group and she was only saying it because the bin was close to Samir and she wanted to SPY on him.

We all watched as Jodi pretended to sharpen her pencil and I KNEW before she even got back to the table

that she'd found out something

BIG

because her face had gone PURE WHITE.

Then Jodi sat down and said, "OK. He's definitely from

OUTER SPACE."

And the whole table started to shake because Maisie was FREAKING OUT.

Zach said, "WHAT DID YOU SEE?!"

And Jodi gulped and said, "He's made a word out of the blocks."

I looked over at baby Samir and he was STARING at us with a little smirk on his face.

And then Jodi said, "He's written MARS!"

Aliens LOVE Shepherd's Pie!

At dinners, we were all still a bit in shock because of the whole MARS THING.

But then Jodi said that that was THE LEAST of our problems because she could smell a smell. A TERRIBLE SMELL. And I thought she was about to say that it was Samir's NAPPY when I smelled the smell too. And it definitely WASN'T a nappy. It was a

MILLION TIMES WORSE

than a stinking, alien-baby nappy because it was the

SHEPHERD'S PIE!

Maisie started to panic and she even got her phone out

and said that she was going to phone the police but we stopped her because the police get VERY ANGRY when you phone them about stuff like

SHEPHERD'S PIE EMERGENCIES.

So anyway, we made Maisie put her phone away and Jodi said that we needed to STAY CALM about the SHEPHERD'S PIE and that we should all breathe IN through our noses and OUT through our mouths because that's what the posters the school nurse had put up after Maisie found the DEAD MOUSE said to do when you were having a PANIC ATTACK.

So we did that and as soon as we started we all realised that it had been a

BAD IDEA

because we were breathing in the disgusting shepherd's pie FUMES and it just made everything worse!

Maisie started to go a bit WOBBLY so I used my tray to fan her face and that helped for a bit but then she spotted something and before I could grab her she fainted and slipped RIGHT under the table.

We all looked over to see what Maisie had seen and that's when Jodi's eyes went WIDE and she said, "NO WAY!"

And we

COULDN'T BELIEVE IT

because the dinner ladies were ALL OVER the baby and they were laughing and feeding him BRIGHT GREEN SPINACH and SHEPHERD'S PIE with a spoon and he was

LOVING IT!

Zach looked a bit like he was going to be sick.

And then he said, "That is NOT NORMAL."

And he was RIGHT because the shepherd's pie at our school is probably the worst food that you get in the whole UNIVERSE and it smells like feet and tastes like SOAP. And the dinner ladies use an ICE-CREAM SCOOP to serve it and we know for a FACT that they don't even wash the scoop before they serve the ice cream (which is disgusting).

We all STARED at the alien baby as he gobbled down the shepherd's pie.

That's when Zach said that the ONLY REASONABLE EXPLANATION was that aliens couldn't TASTE and that they only ate food to SURVIVE and get STRONG.

And I knew that he was right because when I looked over at the baby again he was having SECONDS!

Alien
Phone

That afternoon, our class and some of the Year 5s were taken to do **PAINTING** together with the art teacher, Miss Wood, who sometimes comes to our school.

I really like Miss Wood because she gets mega excited about **ART**. One time when we were supposed to be painting just our hands and doing HAND PRINTS for our "CITIZENS OF THE WORLD" poster, she got really excited because Gary Petrie had painted one side of his face and was pressing it against the poster and she said we could ALL do it, so we did. But then LOADS of parents complained because we went home COVERED in paint and Nola Burke's face went HUGE and she had to go away in an AMBULANCE because she was ALLERGIC to painting her face and we all got a letter home about it and then we didn't see Miss

Wood for a while.

So anyway, when we got to the ACTIVITY BIT we saw that Miss Wood had set up a little display and that Haroon's baby brother was PART of it!

We all STARED at the baby because Miss Wood had dressed him in some sort of TOGA and there was loads of FRUIT all around him and he looked a bit like something from ANCIENT ROME.

Miss Jones laughed when she saw the baby and said that Miss Wood had maybe got a bit CARRIED AWAY AGAIN but we all knew that she **HADN'T** got carried away and that she'd been **MIND CONTROLLED** by the baby and that he had obviously **DEMANDED** the toga **AND** the fruit.

So anyway, we all stood behind the painting easels that Miss Wood had set up and she told us that we should paint a picture of the baby and that what we were doing was called a LIFE painting and that Samir was our LIFE MODEL.

And that's when Zach said, "More like an

and I SWEAR the baby heard him because he whipped his head RIGHT round and STARED at Zach for ages with his **BIG BABY EYES.**

Then Miss Wood put some music on and told us all to **RELAX** and **PAINT WHAT WE SAW,** so we did. And even though I knew I was looking at an **ALIEN BABY** I couldn't help thinking he looked a bit funny and cute actually because he kept trying to dance to the music and he was jiggling about all over the place.

But then Jodi noticed that I was smiling at all the **BABY DANCING** and she came over and inspected my eyes **CLOSELY** to make sure I wasn't having my mind controlled.

Then when it was time for Miss Wood to look at our paintings she walked around saying loads of stuff like, "MAGNIFICENT" and "INSPIRED" and "HEART-BREAKINGLY BEAUTIFUL".

But then when she got to Maisie she didn't say anything. She just called for Miss Jones to come over and Miss Jones bent down and asked Maisie if she was feeling OK and I looked at Maisie's painting and saw that she'd painted an ALIEN with ANTENNAE coming out of its head and THREE EYES and GREEN SLIME pouring out of its ears.

That's when Miss Jones said it was time to stop painting for today and folded Maisie's painting in half even though it hadn't even dried properly yet.

So we all started cleaning up and **THAT'S** when I spotted that the baby had something in his hands and that he was **STARING** at it and **TAPPING** it loads.

So we went over to where Haroon was tidying up his paints and he looked over at the baby and said that it was just his **TOY PHONE** and that Samir took it **EVERYWHERE** with him and that he wouldn't let anyone else touch it and if you tried to take it away from him he would

SCREAM

until you gave it back.

Then Haroon said, "My mum says she doesn't even know where he got it from."

And I gasped and looked at Jodi and her eyes were wide so I knew she was thinking the same thing as me and before I could say a word Jodi said, "That's not a TOY. That's an

ALIEN
COMMUNICATION
DEVICE."

Then Jodi did the HAND SIGNAL which meant FOLLOW ME and ran into the Supply Cupboard. So we waited until Miss Jones wasn't paying attention and sneaked in after her.

We all stood, squashed, in the Supply Cupboard. And that's when

65

Jodi told us that she thought the alien baby was trying to get

BEAMED UP

to an alien SPACESHIP so he could go home to MARS and report back on what he'd found out about our school and life on Earth, and that THAT was why he kept pressing all the buttons on his COMMUNICATION DEVICE.

Then Zach said that it was only a MATTER OF TIME before the MOTHERSHIP arrived and BEAMED HIM UP!

KWASER!

That afternoon, Miss Jones made us stay indoors for a Wet Playtime because it was raining really heavily.

But then the sky got REALLY DARK and Zach said that it must be because the ALIEN MOTHERSHIP had arrived and Maisie had to have a little lie-down on the Reading Rug.

So we asked Miss Jones if we could invite Haroon and his baby brother into OUR class for Wet Playtime and Miss Jones got really excited and said that was a GREAT idea.

And as SOON as Haroon brought the baby into our classroom Miss Jones

JUMPED UP

and took Samir out of his buggy and sat him on her knee and started doing a RAINY DAY QUIZ with us.

I couldn't really concentrate on the quiz because the sky was getting DARKER and Maisie was SHAKING against my leg and Gary Petrie kept shouting out the WRONG ANSWER to every single question with his mouth FULL of crisps because he is .

COMPLETELY
DISGUSTING

and he loves crisps so much that one time when he dropped his last Monster Munch in a puddle some of the boys started chanting, "Eat IT! Eat IT! Eat IT!" and he DID.

Then Haroon nudged me and I
looked and saw that the baby was
STARING at Gary Petrie again.
Then all of a sudden Gary shouted
out an answer and Miss Jones
looked a bit surprised and said,
"Um, yes! That's RIGHT, Gary! Well
done!"

And THAT'S when we noticed
that Samir's eyes had gone

HUGE

and he was opening and shutting
his mouth LOADS and STARING

at Gary and it was obvious that he was sending MESSAGES to Gary's brain.

Then the baby started furiously tapping on his ALIEN PHONE.

And THAT'S when we all heard it. The baby's weird, high-pitched ALIEN VOICE.

At first I couldn't make out what he was saying because of his weird ALIEN VOICE. But then I realised that he was saying the SAME WORD over and over again:

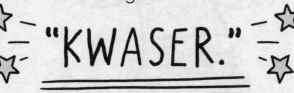

"KWASER."

But then all of a sudden Gary Petrie started CHOKING and Miss Jones put the baby down on the rug and patted Gary on the back until a HUGE crisp came flying out of his mouth and on to the rug.

Then Miss Jones said, "Where's Samir?!"

We all looked at the spot on the rug where Miss Jones had put down the baby but he was GONE!

Then Gary Petrie yelled, "LOOK!" and we all looked and saw Samir's little bottom disappearing out of the classroom door.

Haroon's eyes went WIDE and he said, "He's CRAWLING!"

I looked at Zach and he looked at me because we realised that Samir must be on his way to get BEAMED UP!

SO we all RAN after Samir and

THAT'S when we saw he was crawling REALLY FAST towards the LOCKERS. And then he CRAWLED INSIDE an open one and squealed "KWASER!" at the top of his alien baby LUNGS!

And Zach said, "The LOCKER! That must be the PORTAL to get beamed up to the KWASER MOTHERSHIP!"

And then Haroon screamed, "NOOOOOOOOOOO!"

The Mothership

Haroon **RACED** down the corridor and yelled,

> **"NO! PLEASE DON'T GO!"**

and then he **GRABBED** his baby brother out of the locker.

76

Baby Samir looked a bit surprised and then he SQUEALED with laughter and gave Haroon a big hug.

Mrs Akbar came running out to see what all the fuss was about and Miss Jones told her that Samir had just crawled for the first time and she SCREAMED!

Haroon hugged his baby brother loads and kept saying, "I don't care if you ARE an alien. You're MY brother and I want you to STAY!"

And that's when baby Samir looked RIGHT at Haroon and said, "KWASER" and then he lifted his chubby hand and we all saw that he was holding a packet of QUAVERS!

Then Gary Petrie said, "HEY! Those are MY Quavers out of MY locker!" And then he took the bag of crisps from the baby and started eating them.

The baby's eyes went WIDE and he looked RIGHT at Gary and said, "KWASER, KWASER, KWASER, KWASER!" really fast and Gary Petrie laughed and said, "I gave you one this morning! No more. They're not for babies. They're for MEN!"

And we all BURST out laughing because we realised that the reason

the baby had been STARING at Gary all day and saying "KWASER" was because he wanted one of Gary Petrie's crisps!

Then Mrs Akbar RUSHED over and said, "I can't believe this! My big boy! You've CRAWLED for the first time AND said your FIRST WORD in the same day!"

And the baby said, "KWASER!"

So Gary Petrie gave up and handed Samir a Quaver and he SQUEALED with delight and started sucking on it LOADS.

But then Mrs Akbar tried to take the crisp away and Samir started

so she gave it back to him and said,
"OK. But just ONE."

We all watched as the baby
sucked on the Quaver with WIDE
EYES until it got all wet and gooey
and then he took it out of his mouth
and handed it to Haroon and said,
"HAROO."

Maisie gasped and said, "He's trying to say Haroon!"

Mrs Akbar clapped her hands together and started screaming a bit again.

And Haroon did the

BIGGEST

smile I have ever seen and gave his baby brother another hug (but he didn't eat the soggy Quaver).

Then Mrs Akbar asked Miss Jones to look after the baby and she took Haroon away into one of the classrooms for a bit.

We had

NO IDEA

what was going on but then a few
minutes later Haroon came out
and said that his mum had had a
little talk with him and asked him
why he'd called his brother an
ALIEN and that he had told her
EVERYTHING.

Haroon said his mum had got a bit
upset and that she'd said she was
sorry she hadn't realised that he had
been feeling left out. And then she
said she was just **TIRED** because

babies are HARD WORK and that she was going to make it up to him and that the baby definitely wasn't controlling her mind with alien powers.

Then Haroon told us that the baby had been keeping his mum awake at night, too, and that she thought maybe Samir was LONELY in a room by himself because he LOVED being around people and he probably found it hard being on his own at night time.

Haroon said that he'd asked his mum if Samir could share HIS room for a while to see if that helped because he didn't want his baby brother to be lonely and that made her really happy and she'd said yes.

Then Maisie said, "So he's **NOT** using

ALIEN
MIND
CONTROL?"

And Haroon said that he wasn't and that his mum told him **ALL** babies are able to control people a little bit and that doesn't mean they're aliens from outer space.

But then Jodi said, "What about the blocks?"

85

And Haroon said that it was just a

COINCIDENCE

that Samir had spelled "MARS".

But then Zach said, "What about his **ALIEN PHONE?**"

And Jodi nodded loads and said that we needed to **INSPECT** the

ALIEN
COMMUNICATION
DEVICE

to be one hundred per cent sure, and we all agreed.

So we went over to where Mrs Akbar was speaking to Miss Jones and Haroon bent down next to Samir's pram and pointed to the phone in his hand and said, "Can Haroo have? Please?" and reached out for it.

And Samir smiled and said, "HAROOOOOO" and gave him the phone and we all knew that the baby really LOVED Haroon because he never let ANYONE touch his phone.

So we all INSPECTED the phone and there were no wires or lights and there was even a hole at the bottom that you could see into and when we looked inside, the phone was completely HOLLOW.

THAT'S when we all knew for SURE that we'd got it WRONG and that Haroon's baby brother WASN'T from outer space and that he was just a chatty baby who loved his toy phone and was a bit obsessed with crisps.

Then Jodi said that the INVESTIGATION was

OFFICIALLY CLOSED

and that Haroon should ERASE the location of The Den from his memory and Haroon laughed and said he would try.

At the end of the day, Haroon brought Samir to say goodbye to us all and Maisie asked if she could hold him and we were

SHOCKED

because we thought Maisie was TERRIFIED of babies!

But Maisie said that she wasn't scared of Samir and that he was CUTE and she even kissed his chubby cheek and made his eyes go wide and he said, "KWASER" and we all laughed.

Then Jodi said that she wanted to hold him too and that it was time she got over her

TRAUMATIC EXPERIENCE.

So Haroon passed the baby to Jodi and as SOON as he did we all heard a WEIRD SOUND and Jodi's eyes went WIDE and Haroon said, "Uh-oh. I think he needs his nappy changed!"

Samir started WRIGGLING and the nappy came LOOSE and FELL

OFF on to the ground!

Jodi SCREAMED and Maisie FAINTED.

Zach looked at the nappy and said, "That is NOT NORMAL for a HUMAN baby!"

And he was RIGHT.

Because it was BRIGHT GREEN.

It was an

☆ ☆ ☆ ☆ ☆

ALIEN POO FROM OUTER SPACE!

☆ ☆ ☆ ☆ ☆

And we all GASPED.

OTHER AMAZING BOOKS BY PAMELA BUTCHART!

Illustrated by

THOMAS FLINTHAM

Illustrated by GEMMA CORRELL

Illustrated by BECKA MOOR

Why not try another fantastic
Nosy Crow book?

MAX
The
DETECTIVE CAT

The
DISAPPEARING
DIVA

illustrated by
NICOLA KINNEAR

Sarah Todd Taylor

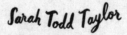

CHAPTER 1
The Rooftops of London

Maximilian peered through the basket at the oily river and wrinkled his powdered nose. The smell of the city was harsh and sour, and everywhere seemed to be made of noise. He was not used to this.

Maximilian was used to silver dishes, velvet cushions and the very finest salmon soufflé. Maximilian was used to his beloved Countess Arlington fussing over him at least six times a day and eight times on Saturdays. Maximilian was *not* used to being stuffed into a smelly cat basket and sent off with one of the maids, late at night and without so much as a sniff of his supper.

The maid in question, a rather clumsy girl with rosy cheeks, pressed her face to the basket. Maximilian fixed her with what he hoped was a regal stare and miaowed his "a terrible mistake has been made, take me back home at once" miaow.

The girl made little shushing noises. "Don't worry, you silly scrap," she whispered. "I'm not really going to drown you, no matter what she says."

Maximilian frowned. He didn't know what drowning was, but the way the girl said it made him think it wasn't something nice like salmon mousse or tummy tickles. He could not think why the silly child had brought him out on such a cold, damp night to sit by a smelly river. Countess Arlington would be worrying about him by now. Maximilian started to scratch at the basket, taking care not to snag any of his beautiful fur.

The girl looked out over the river. "I don't know quite what I'm going to do with you though," she said. "And I have to go back soon."

Maximilian let out a low, rather ungentlemanly growl and lay down with his chin on his paws. It was rude to growl, but the girl was being extremely stupid. Everyone, in fact, had been behaving rather stupidly today, ever since his little adventure with the soil and the mouse and the maid.

Maximilian lived in Arlington Grove, the most fashionable townhouse in London. To be precise, Maximilian lived on a red velvet cushion in the drawing room of Arlington Grove, the most fashionable townhouse in London. His cushion was set into the window seat to catch the afternoon sun and was extremely comfortable, but he had never seen the rest of the house.

Until this morning.

This morning the maid had left the drawing-room door ajar after changing the pink roses in the vases and Maximilian had followed her out and explored. He found a spider in a plant pot and pounced on it, scattering soil across the cream carpets. He left muddy footprints on the crisp white bed sheets in the guest rooms. He scampered down a long staircase to the kitchens, where he had great fun chasing some mice till one ran into the middle of the room and a maid holding a pan full of fat screamed and dropped it all over him.

Maximilian was quickly returned to the drawing room, covered in soil and dripping with greasy fat. Countess Arlington took one look at him, shrieked and ordered him to be washed with disinfecting soap that stung his eyes and got into his nose and ears. Clean and dry, he was put back on his cushion to sit quietly while the maids fussed around, clearing up the mess he had made.

Later on, the butler had stuffed him into the cat basket and the maid had brought him down to the river.

Maximilian stared at the girl, who was looking from side to side as if deciding what to do. He was getting colder and damper and had had rather enough of being cried at. It was time to take matters into his own paws. Somewhere out in the city was his home and Countess Arlington, and Maximilian wanted to be in that somewhere, not trapped in a basket by a smelly river.

The cat basket was held shut by a small bar threaded through two loops on the front. Maximilian squeezed a paw through the latticed willow of the basket, wincing as a sharp piece of wood scratched the soft pad on his paw. After a little wiggling he managed to get close to the bar. He gave it a little tap and, as it clattered to the ground, sprang at the basket's lid. It flew open and he leapt out. He heard a gasp behind him, but there was no time to lose and, ignoring the girl's cries of

"Come back, you silly puss!" Maximilian fled as fast as he could into the night.

The city at night was a very different place from one cushioned and perfumed room. For one thing, there seemed to be feet everywhere. Rough, booted feet that kicked out at him, hobnailed clogs that threatened to crush his tail, daintily shod feet in T-bar shoes that stepped quickly away in alarm as he dashed past.

The streets were packed to bursting. Maximilian could not believe how noisy the world was. Sounds came at him from every direction, and all of them were harsh and not at all welcoming to a cat on his own for the first time in his life.

He ran till his paws were red and sore, and then he looked for a place to hide and rest. The city was a most confusing place. Whichever way he went seemed to lead back to the river, a great expanse of water that glistened in the moonlight and smelled like. . . Maximilian tried to think of what it smelled like, but his whole life he had been surrounded by perfume and talcum and dried pieces of flower called potpourri. The only smell he knew he didn't like was flea powder and even *that* smelled better than this. It was a smell that had something fishy in it, but not the sort of fish that Maximilian thought he would want to eat.

Maximilian decided to ignore the fact that his tummy was feeling empty. There was a bridge a little way ahead of him and a cat might, if a cat were lucky, find somewhere soft to lie down. He was tired and had missed at least two of his daily catnaps, so it was time to catch up.

There was nothing soft to lie down on under the bridge, only hard brickwork and dust that made Maximilian shudder with dismay. How he wished that he was back on his comfy window cushion, with the soft velvet pile that lay in just the right direction for his fur. He padded around, testing the ground with a paw to see if there was anywhere that was clean.

"Well, pick a place and be quick about it," said a voice somewhere in the dark. "Some of us have been hunting all day."

Maximilian froze. The maids at Arlington Grove had been very fond of telling him he was spoiled and that out in what they called "the real world" cats were not treated as well as he was. One rather spiteful girl in particular would delight in holding him up to the window to point out stray cats in the street below. They looked scruffy and ill cared for with their scraggy tails and matted fur.

"Proper cats, that's what they are. Not pampered balls of fluff. They'd make mincemeat of you, my lad," the girl would say, shaking Maximilian so roughly that his fur would feel quite out of sorts.

What if this were one of those strays, come to make mincemeat of him?

WORLD
BOOK
DAY

Hello

We hope you enjoyed this book.

Proudly brought to you by **WORLD BOOK DAY,**

the **BIGGEST CELEBRATION** of the **magic** and **fun** of **storytelling.**

We are the **bringer of books to readers** everywhere

and a **charity** on a **MISSION**

to take you on a **READING JOURNEY.**

EXPLORE new worlds (and bookshops!)

EXPAND your imagination

DISCOVER some of the very best authors and illustrators with us.

A **LOVE OF READING** is one of life's greatest gifts.

And this book is **OUR gift to YOU.**

HAPPY READING.
HAPPY WORLD BOOK DAY!

WORLD BOOK DAY

SHARE A STORY

Discover and share stories from breakfast to bedtime.

THREE ways to continue **YOUR** reading adventure

1 VISIT YOUR LOCAL BOOKSHOP

Your go-to destination for awesome reading recommendations and events with your favourite authors and illustrators.

FIND YOUR LOCAL BOOKSHOP

booksellers.org.uk/bookshopsearch

2 JOIN YOUR LOCAL LIBRARY

Browse and borrow from a huge selection of books, get expert ideas of what to read next and take part in wonderful family reading activities – all for FREE!

FIND YOUR LOCAL LIBRARY

findmylibrary.co.uk

3 GO ONLINE AT WORLDBOOKDAY.COM

Fun podcasts, activities, games, videos, downloads, competitions, new books galore and all the latest book news.

SPONSORED B

NATIONAL **BOOK** tokens

Celebrate stories. Love reading.